Ellie
and the
Sunflowers

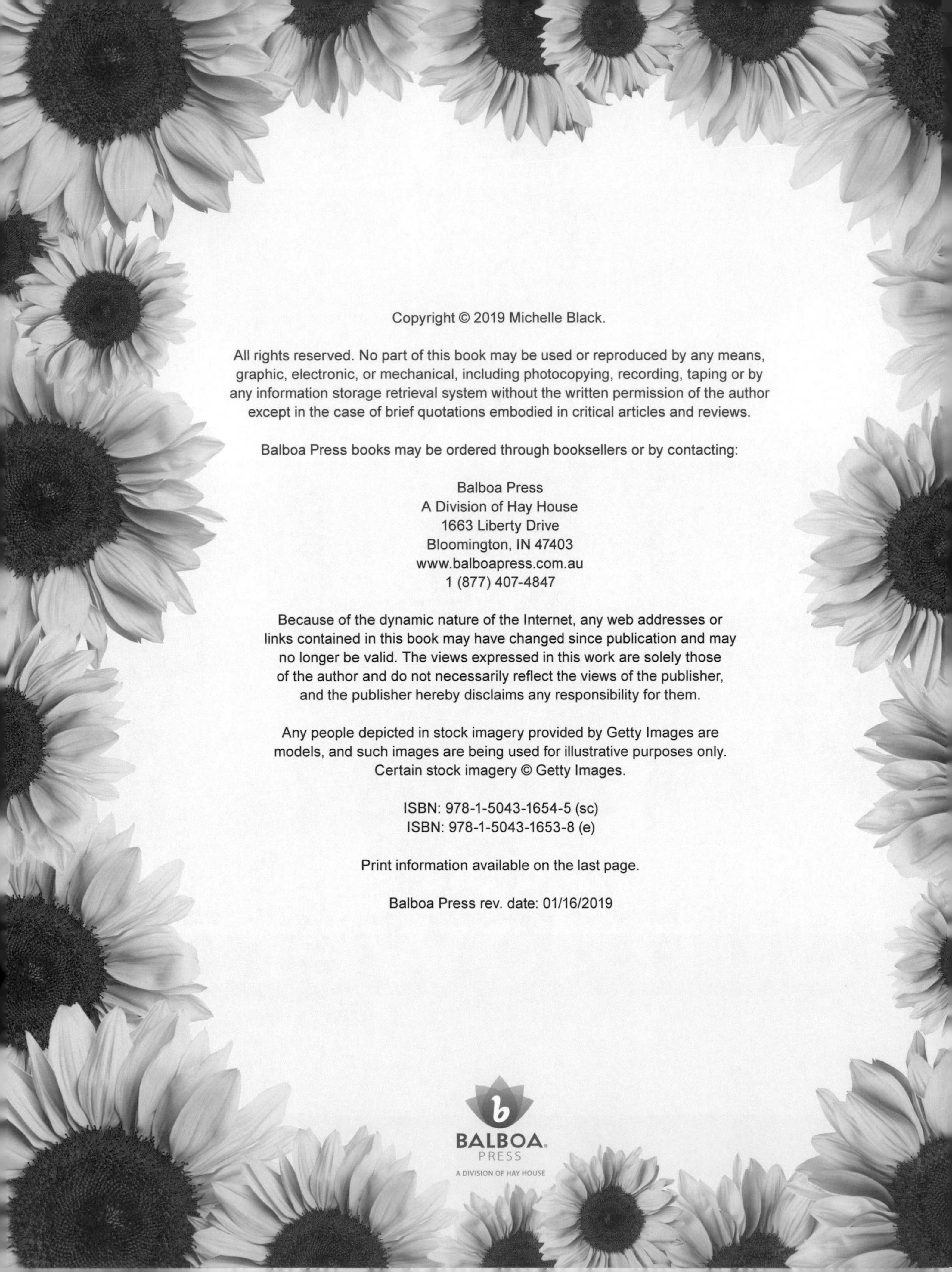

Balboa Press books may be ordered through booksellers or by contacting:

Balboa Press
A Division of Hay House
1663 Liberty Drive
Bloomington, IN 47403
www.balboapress.com.au
1 (877) 407-4847

ISBN: 978-1-5043-1654-5 (sc)
ISBN: 978-1-5043-1653-8 (e)

Print information available on the last page.

Balboa Press rev. date: 01/16/2019

Acknowledgement

This book is presented with much gratitude to the clinicians and researchers that continue to uncover new evidence to balance the mind and body, of special note I acknowledge the research for: a) Presence and body posture, A. Cuddy; b) Mindfulness Based Stress Reduction, J. Kabot-Zin; and c) Psychophysiology of stress and heart brain coherence, R.McCraty.

I am forever grateful to our wonderful son Perry for his encouragement, unconditional love, passion for horses and commitment to following his dreams; my husband Jason for the unique relationship and life we share; and my big brother Paul for always listening, encouraging and checking-in.

To my good friends, family and mentors who have been part of my experience, listened, understood, misunderstood, laughed, celebrated, commiserated and encouraged, thank you.

To all who care for children, thank you for caring, this book is for you to share.

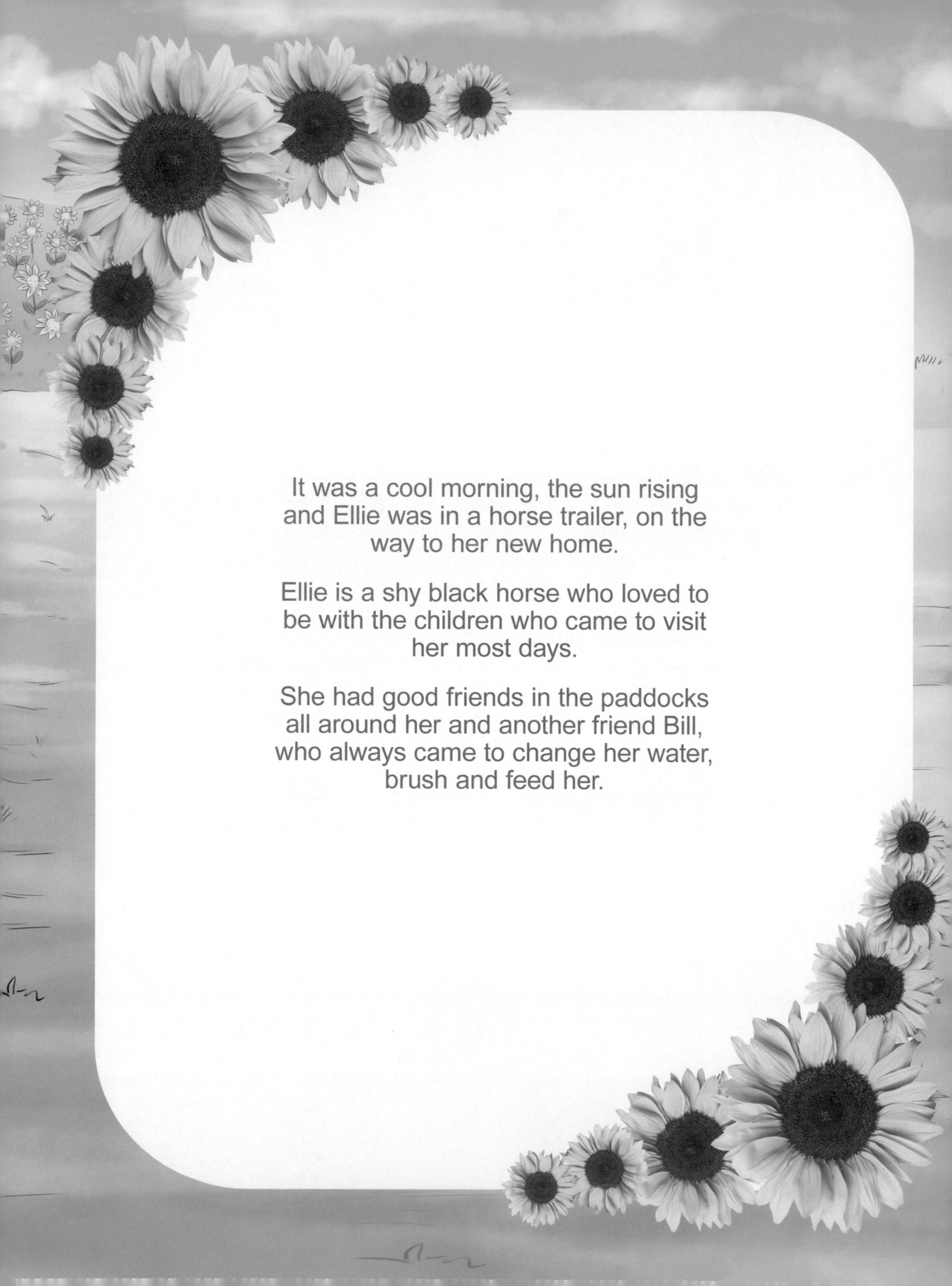

It was a cool morning, the sun rising and Ellie was in a horse trailer, on the way to her new home.

Ellie is a shy black horse who loved to be with the children who came to visit her most days.

She had good friends in the paddocks all around her and another friend Bill, who always came to change her water, brush and feed her.

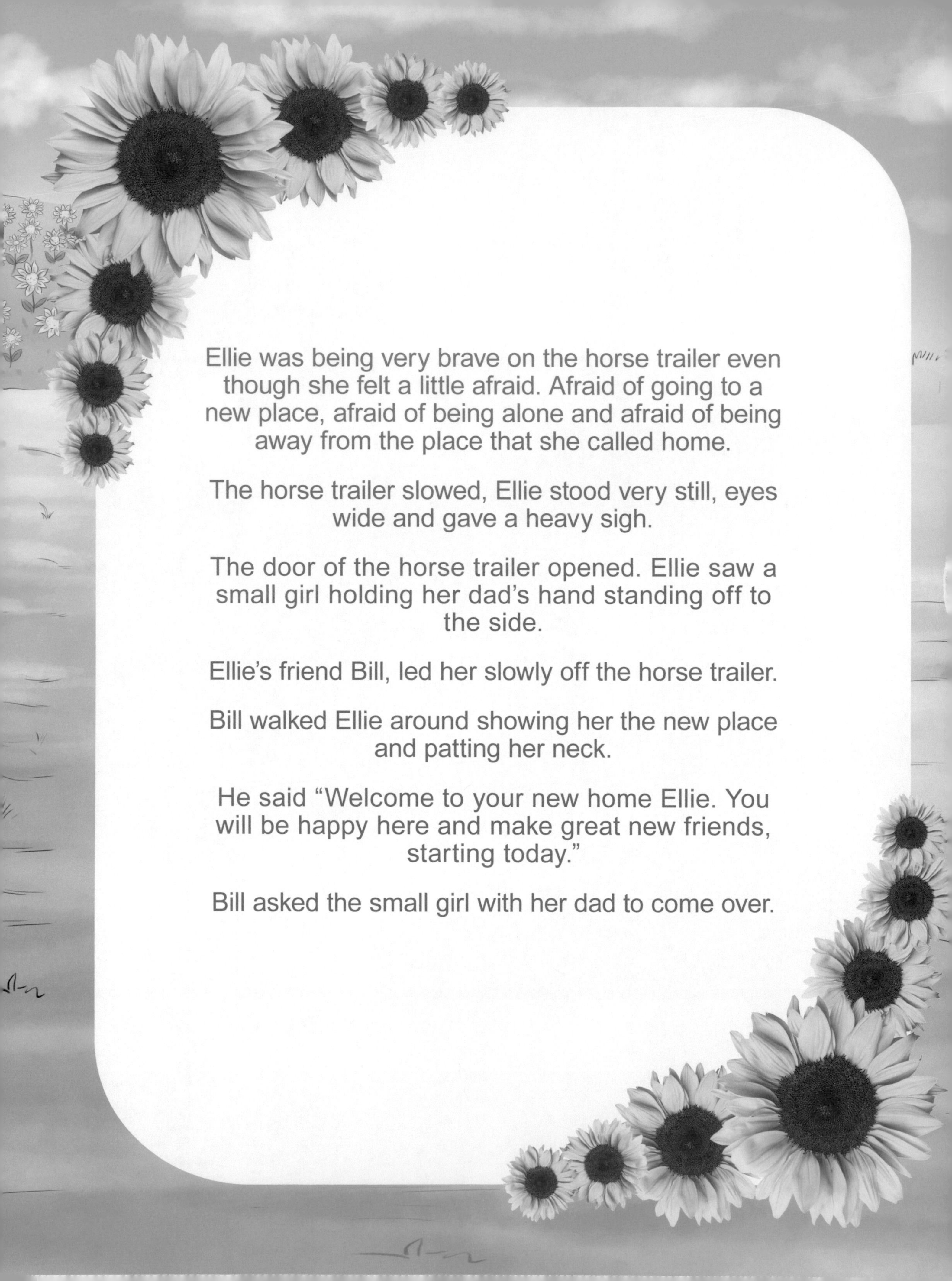

Ellie was being very brave on the horse trailer even though she felt a little afraid. Afraid of going to a new place, afraid of being alone and afraid of being away from the place that she called home.

The horse trailer slowed, Ellie stood very still, eyes wide and gave a heavy sigh.

The door of the horse trailer opened. Ellie saw a small girl holding her dad's hand standing off to the side.

Ellie's friend Bill, led her slowly off the horse trailer.

Bill walked Ellie around showing her the new place and patting her neck.

He said "Welcome to your new home Ellie. You will be happy here and make great new friends, starting today."

Bill asked the small girl with her dad to come over.

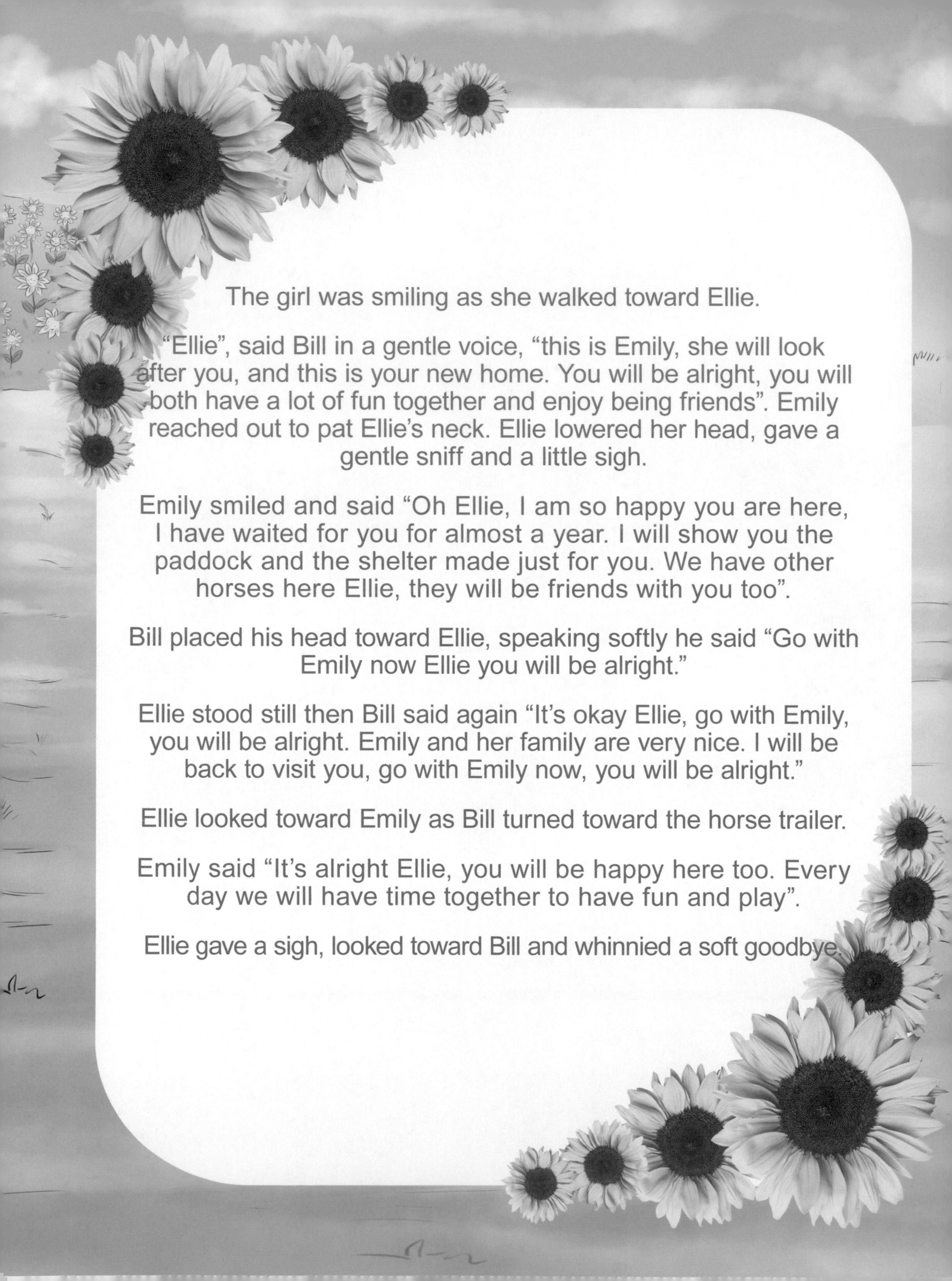

The girl was smiling as she walked toward Ellie.

"Ellie", said Bill in a gentle voice, "this is Emily, she will look after you, and this is your new home. You will be alright, you will both have a lot of fun together and enjoy being friends". Emily reached out to pat Ellie's neck. Ellie lowered her head, gave a gentle sniff and a little sigh.

Emily smiled and said "Oh Ellie, I am so happy you are here, I have waited for you for almost a year. I will show you the paddock and the shelter made just for you. We have other horses here Ellie, they will be friends with you too".

Bill placed his head toward Ellie, speaking softly he said "Go with Emily now Ellie you will be alright."

Ellie stood still then Bill said again "It's okay Ellie, go with Emily, you will be alright. Emily and her family are very nice. I will be back to visit you, go with Emily now, you will be alright."

Ellie looked toward Emily as Bill turned toward the horse trailer.

Emily said "It's alright Ellie, you will be happy here too. Every day we will have time together to have fun and play".

Ellie gave a sigh, looked toward Bill and whinnied a soft goodbye.

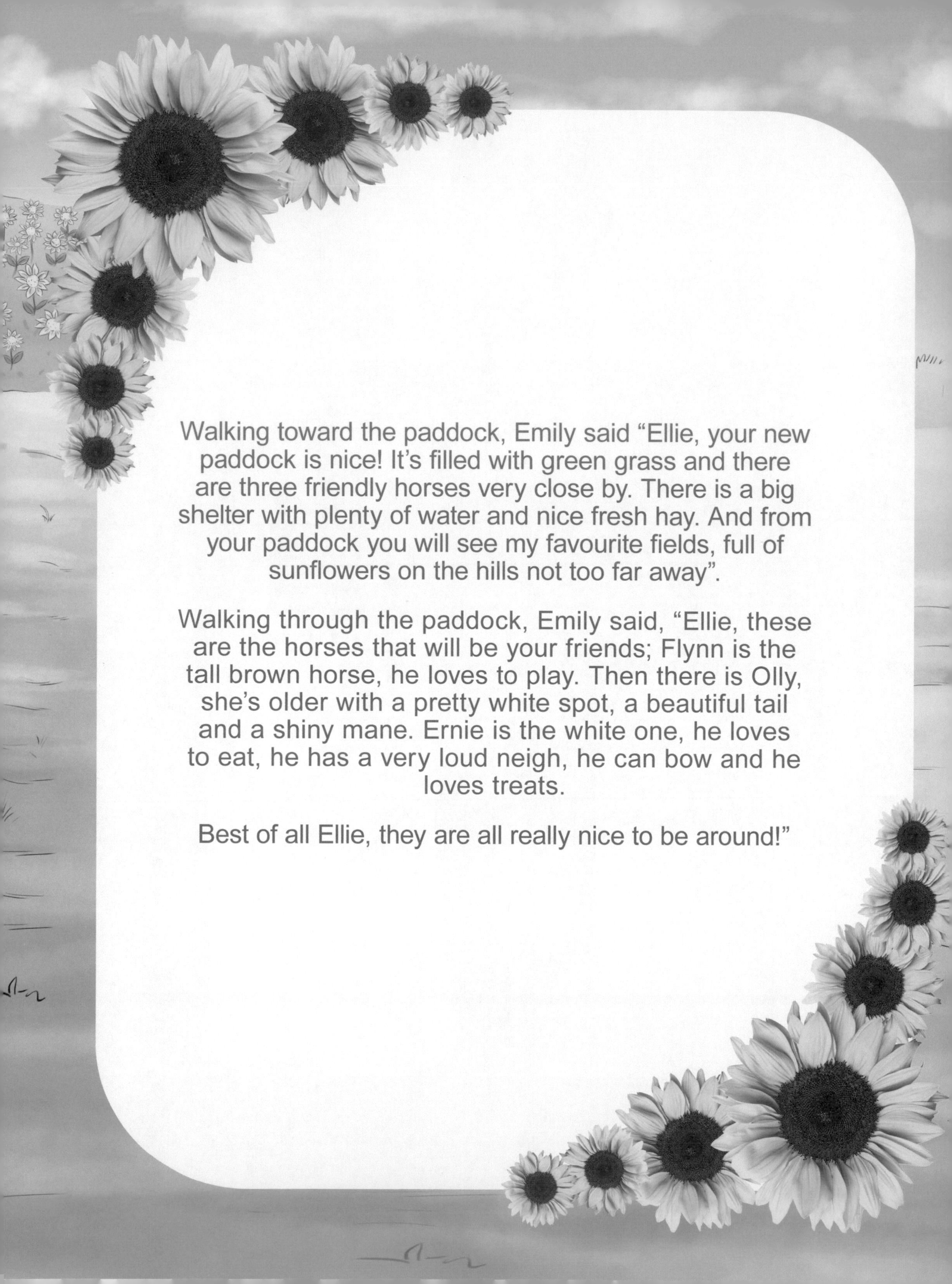

Walking toward the paddock, Emily said “Ellie, your new paddock is nice! It’s filled with green grass and there are three friendly horses very close by. There is a big shelter with plenty of water and nice fresh hay. And from your paddock you will see my favourite fields, full of sunflowers on the hills not too far away”.

Walking through the paddock, Emily said, “Ellie, these are the horses that will be your friends; Flynn is the tall brown horse, he loves to play. Then there is Olly, she’s older with a pretty white spot, a beautiful tail and a shiny mane. Ernie is the white one, he loves to eat, he has a very loud neigh, he can bow and he loves treats.

Best of all Ellie, they are all really nice to be around!”

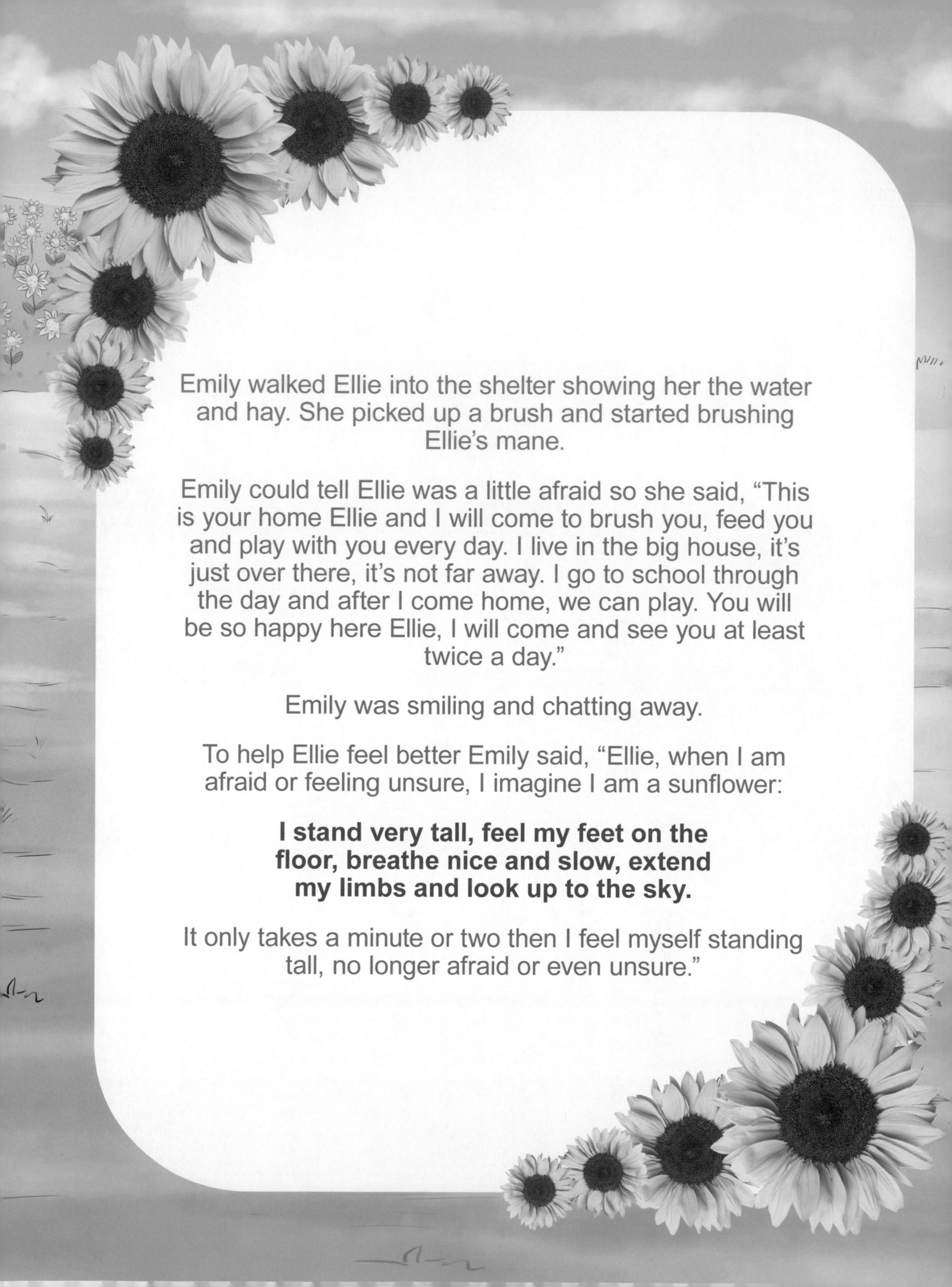

Emily walked Ellie into the shelter showing her the water and hay. She picked up a brush and started brushing Ellie's mane.

Emily could tell Ellie was a little afraid so she said, "This is your home Ellie and I will come to brush you, feed you and play with you every day. I live in the big house, it's just over there, it's not far away. I go to school through the day and after I come home, we can play. You will be so happy here Ellie, I will come and see you at least twice a day."

Emily was smiling and chatting away.

To help Ellie feel better Emily said, "Ellie, when I am afraid or feeling unsure, I imagine I am a sunflower:

I stand very tall, feel my feet on the floor, breathe nice and slow, extend my limbs and look up to the sky.

It only takes a minute or two then I feel myself standing tall, no longer afraid or even unsure."

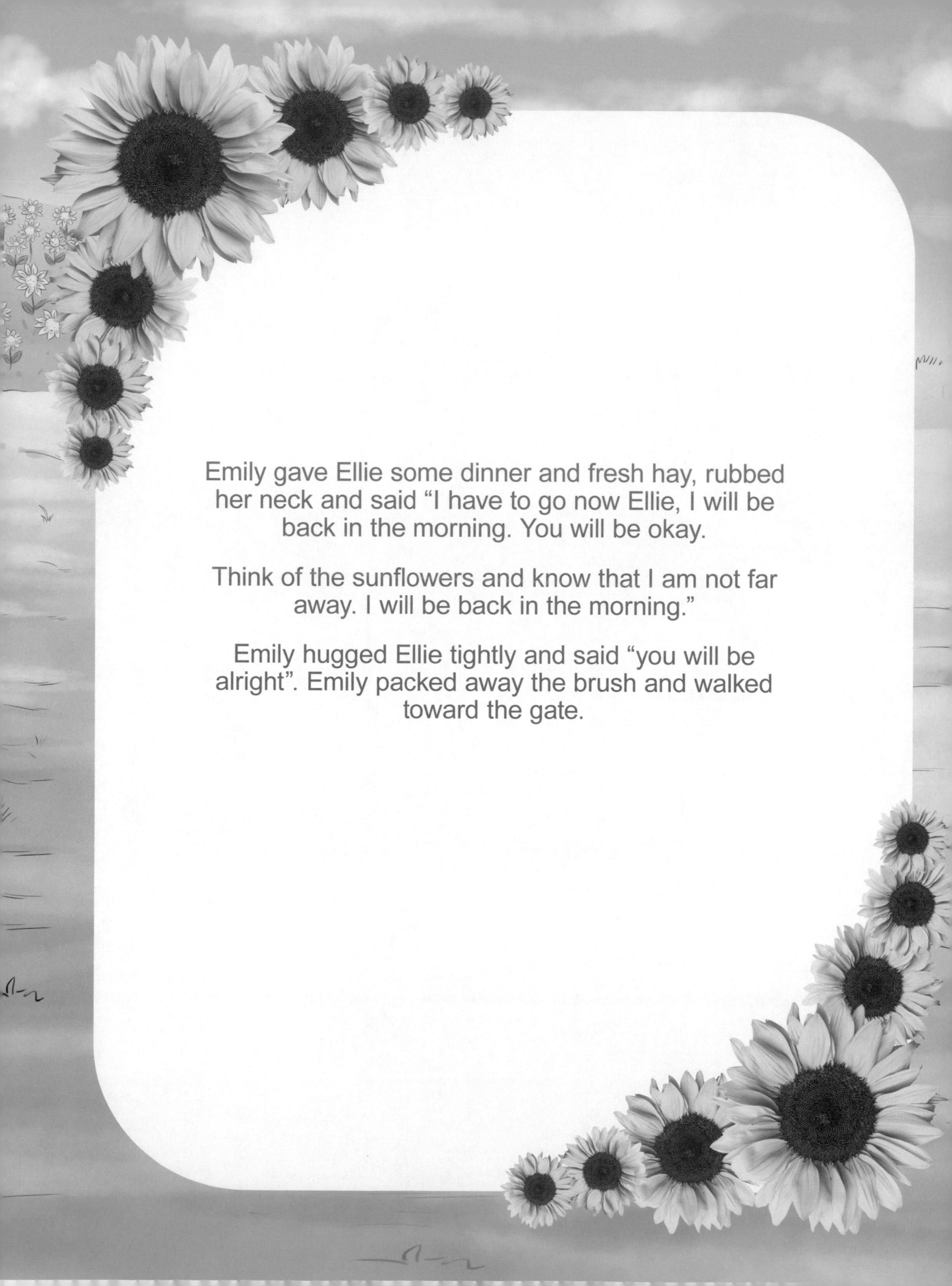

Emily gave Ellie some dinner and fresh hay, rubbed her neck and said “I have to go now Ellie, I will be back in the morning. You will be okay.

Think of the sunflowers and know that I am not far away. I will be back in the morning.”

Emily hugged Ellie tightly and said “you will be alright”. Emily packed away the brush and walked toward the gate.

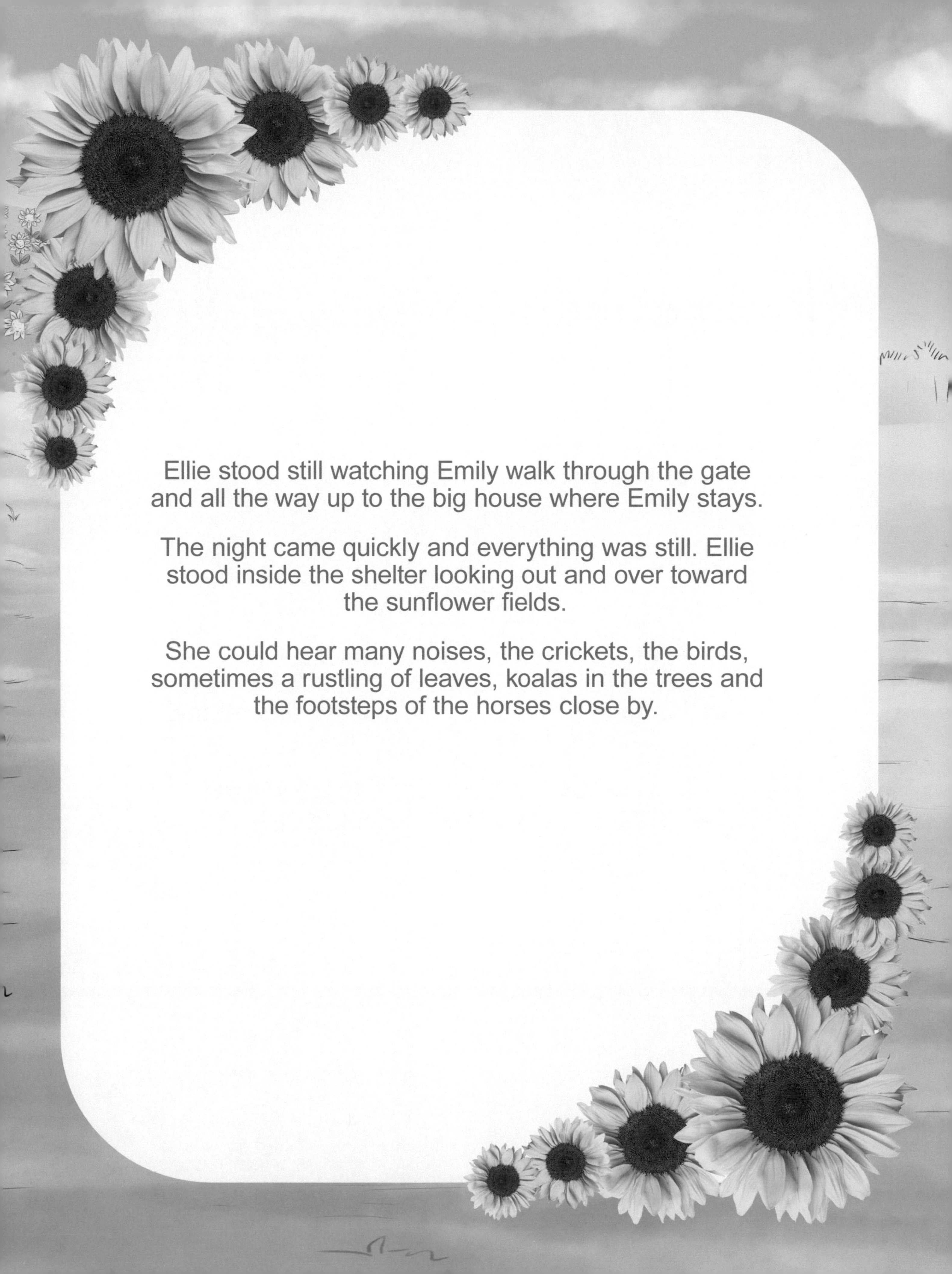

Ellie stood still watching Emily walk through the gate and all the way up to the big house where Emily stays.

The night came quickly and everything was still. Ellie stood inside the shelter looking out and over toward the sunflower fields.

She could hear many noises, the crickets, the birds, sometimes a rustling of leaves, koalas in the trees and the footsteps of the horses close by.

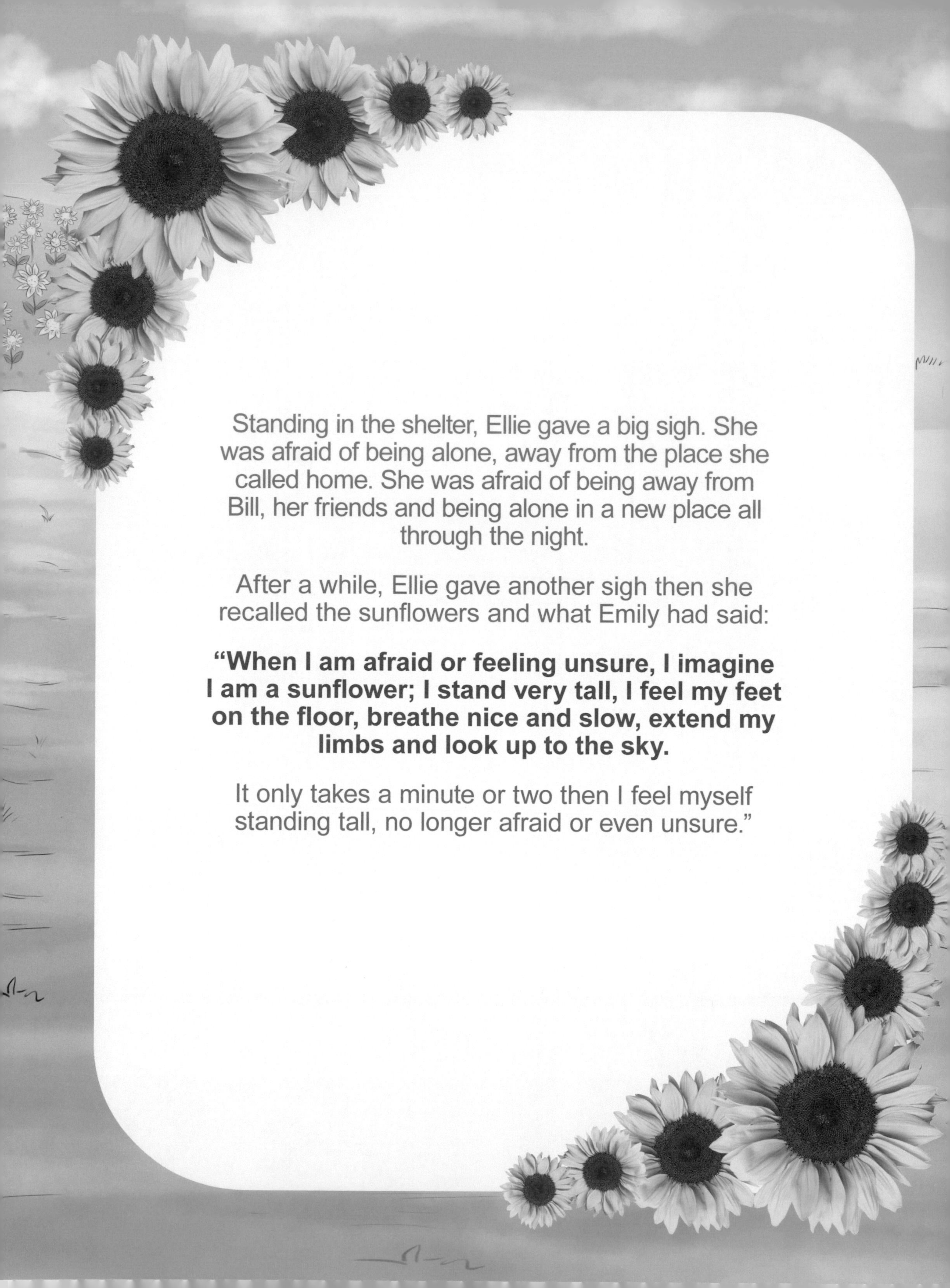

Standing in the shelter, Ellie gave a big sigh. She was afraid of being alone, away from the place she called home. She was afraid of being away from Bill, her friends and being alone in a new place all through the night.

After a while, Ellie gave another sigh then she recalled the sunflowers and what Emily had said:

“When I am afraid or feeling unsure, I imagine I am a sunflower; I stand very tall, I feel my feet on the floor, breathe nice and slow, extend my limbs and look up to the sky.

It only takes a minute or two then I feel myself standing tall, no longer afraid or even unsure.”

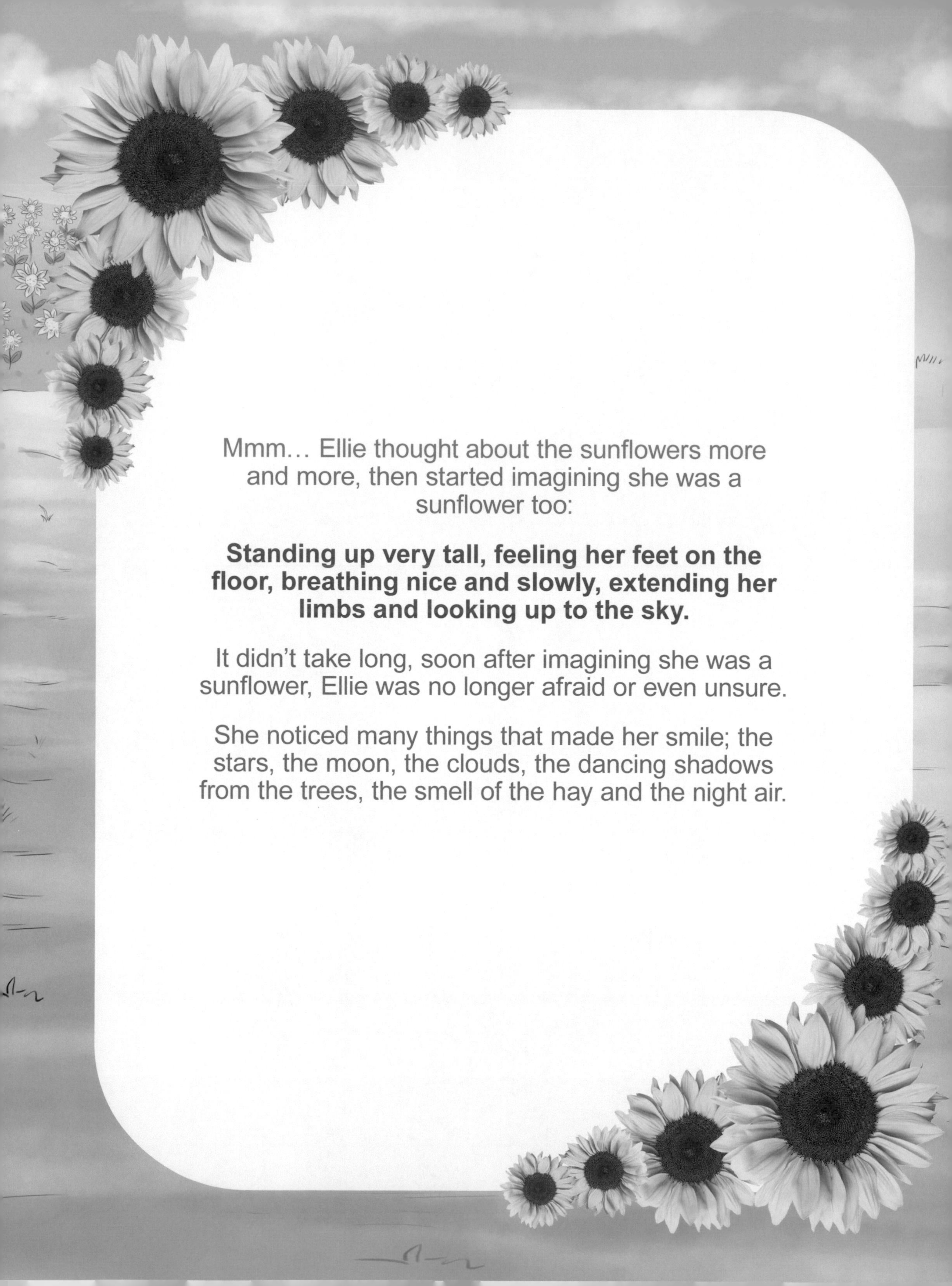

Mmm… Ellie thought about the sunflowers more and more, then started imagining she was a sunflower too:

Standing up very tall, feeling her feet on the floor, breathing nice and slowly, extending her limbs and looking up to the sky.

It didn't take long, soon after imagining she was a sunflower, Ellie was no longer afraid or even unsure.

She noticed many things that made her smile; the stars, the moon, the clouds, the dancing shadows from the trees, the smell of the hay and the night air.

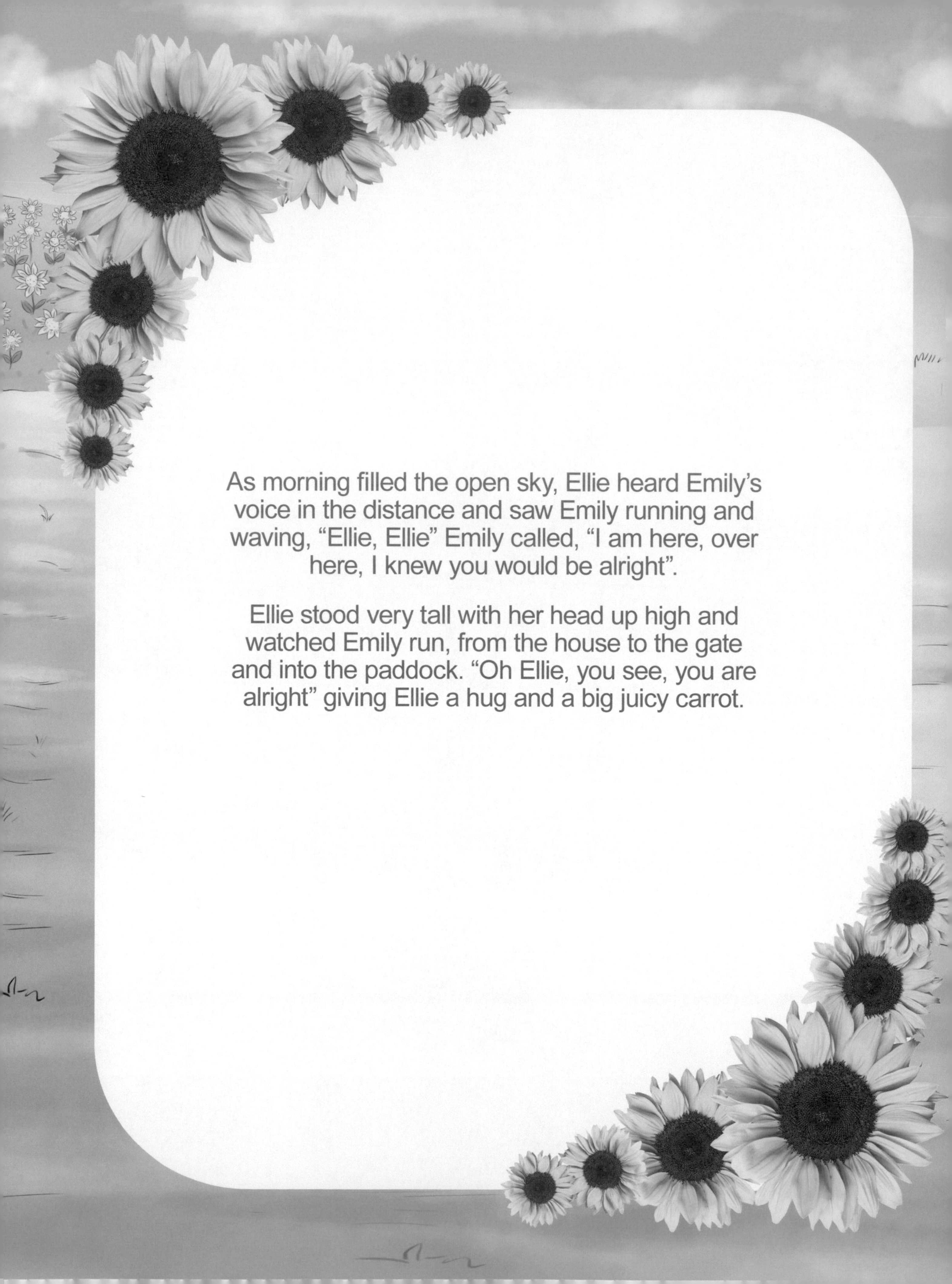

As morning filled the open sky, Ellie heard Emily's voice in the distance and saw Emily running and waving, "Ellie, Ellie" Emily called, "I am here, over here, I knew you would be alright".

Ellie stood very tall with her head up high and watched Emily run, from the house to the gate and into the paddock. "Oh Ellie, you see, you are alright" giving Ellie a hug and a big juicy carrot.

Chatting away, just like she promised, Emily gave Ellie a brush all over, filled her water and gave her more fresh hay.

She gave Ellie a big hug and said “I’ll be back this afternoon, after school, then we can play. Oh Ellie, have a good day”.

Ellie stood up tall and watched Emily run, back toward the house, in then out and a little further away. Onto the bus and then on her way.

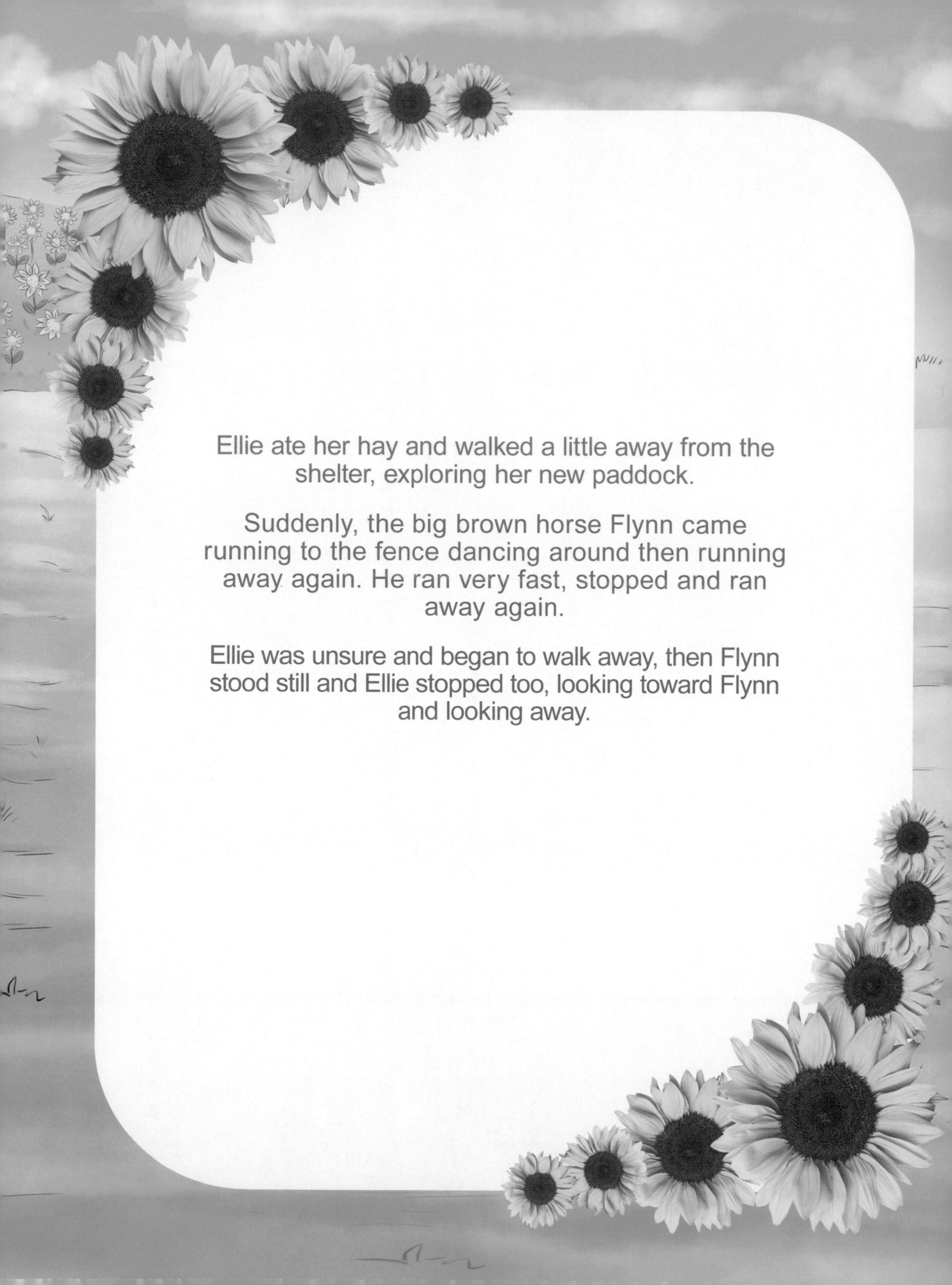

Ellie ate her hay and walked a little away from the shelter, exploring her new paddock.

Suddenly, the big brown horse Flynn came running to the fence dancing around then running away again. He ran very fast, stopped and ran away again.

Ellie was unsure and began to walk away, then Flynn stood still and Ellie stopped too, looking toward Flynn and looking away.

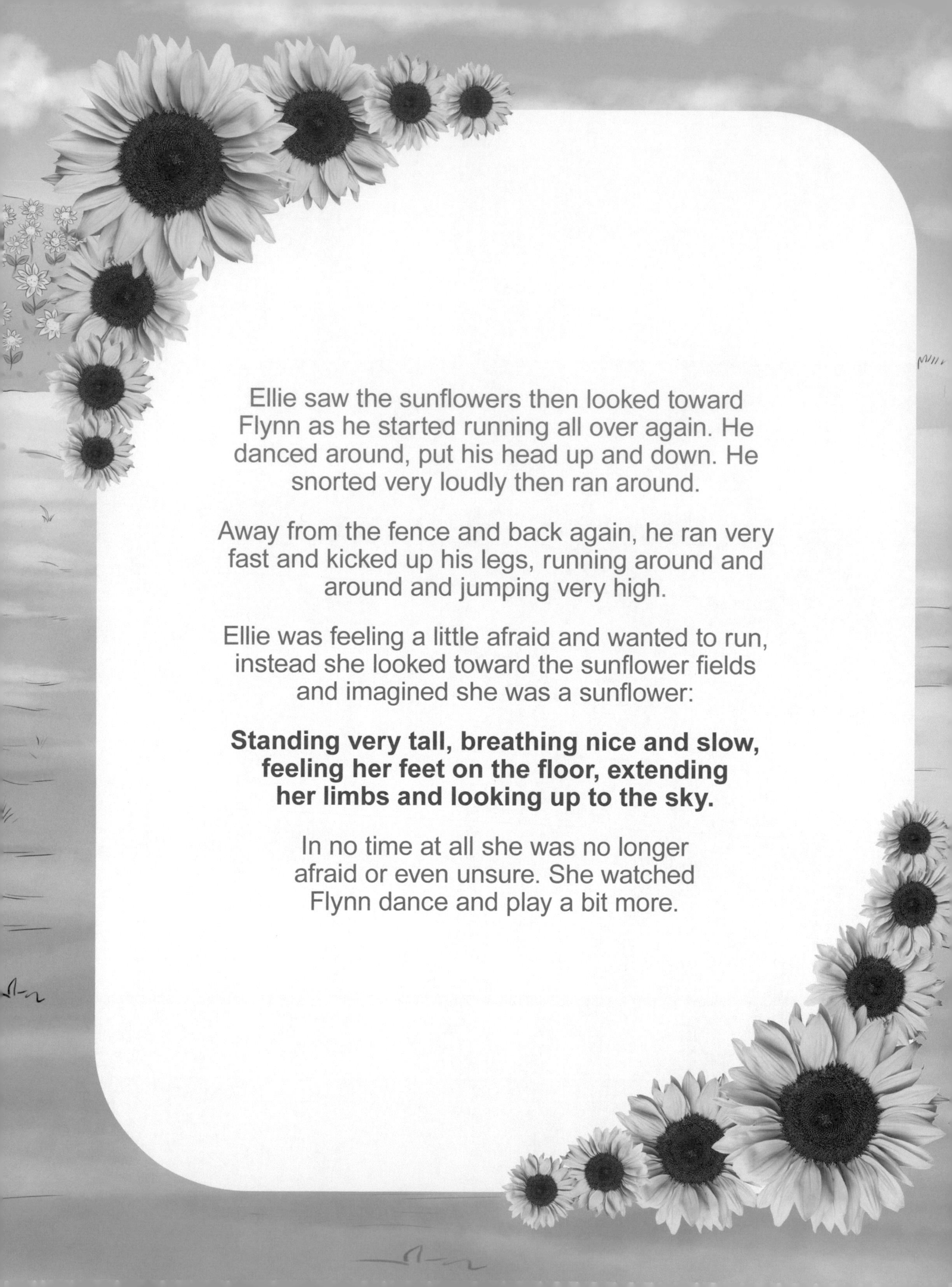

Ellie saw the sunflowers then looked toward Flynn as he started running all over again. He danced around, put his head up and down. He snorted very loudly then ran around.

Away from the fence and back again, he ran very fast and kicked up his legs, running around and around and jumping very high.

Ellie was feeling a little afraid and wanted to run, instead she looked toward the sunflower fields and imagined she was a sunflower:

Standing very tall, breathing nice and slow, feeling her feet on the floor, extending her limbs and looking up to the sky.

In no time at all she was no longer afraid or even unsure. She watched Flynn dance and play a bit more.

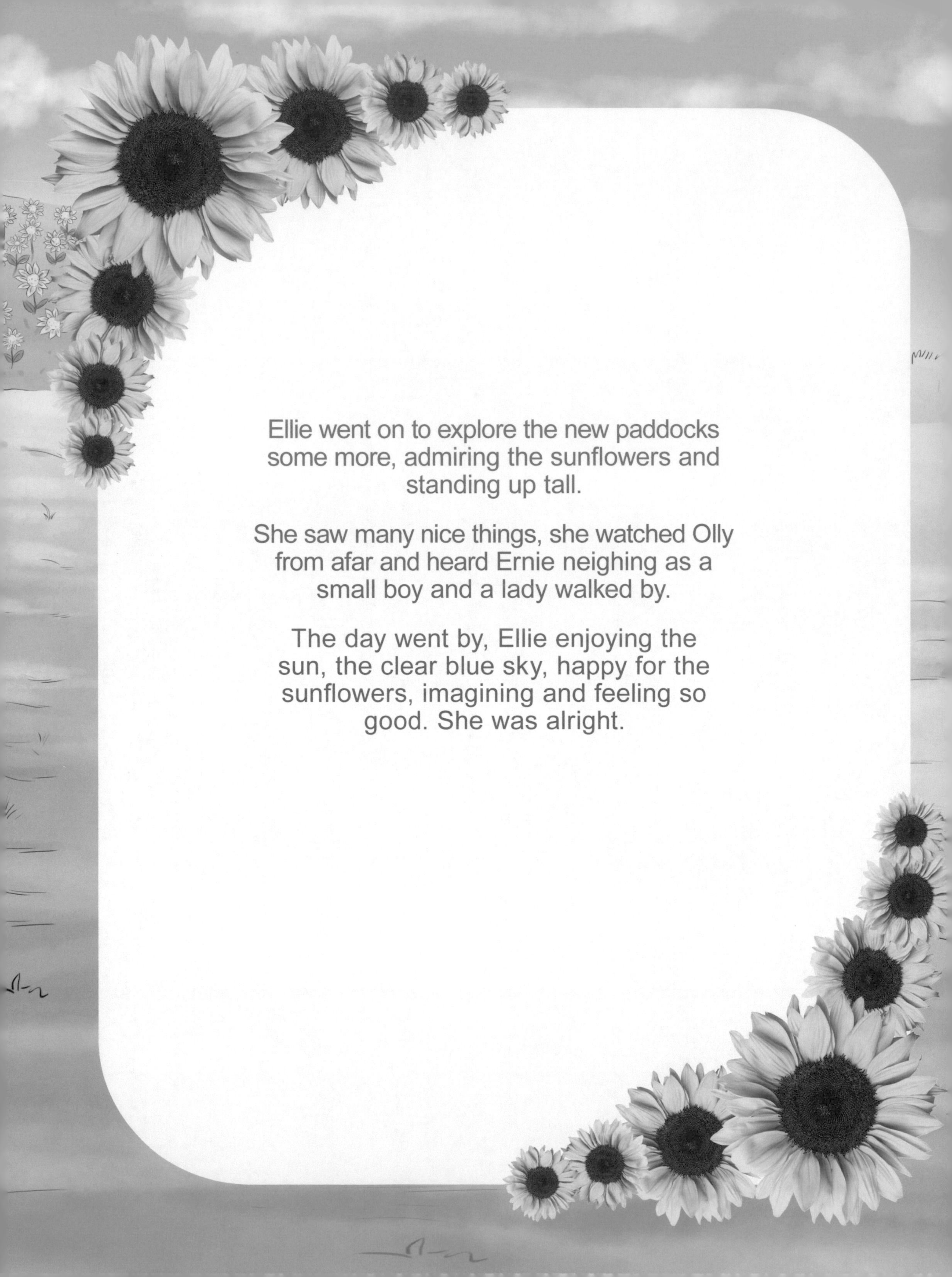

Ellie went on to explore the new paddocks some more, admiring the sunflowers and standing up tall.

She saw many nice things, she watched Olly from afar and heard Ernie neighing as a small boy and a lady walked by.

The day went by, Ellie enjoying the sun, the clear blue sky, happy for the sunflowers, imagining and feeling so good. She was alright.

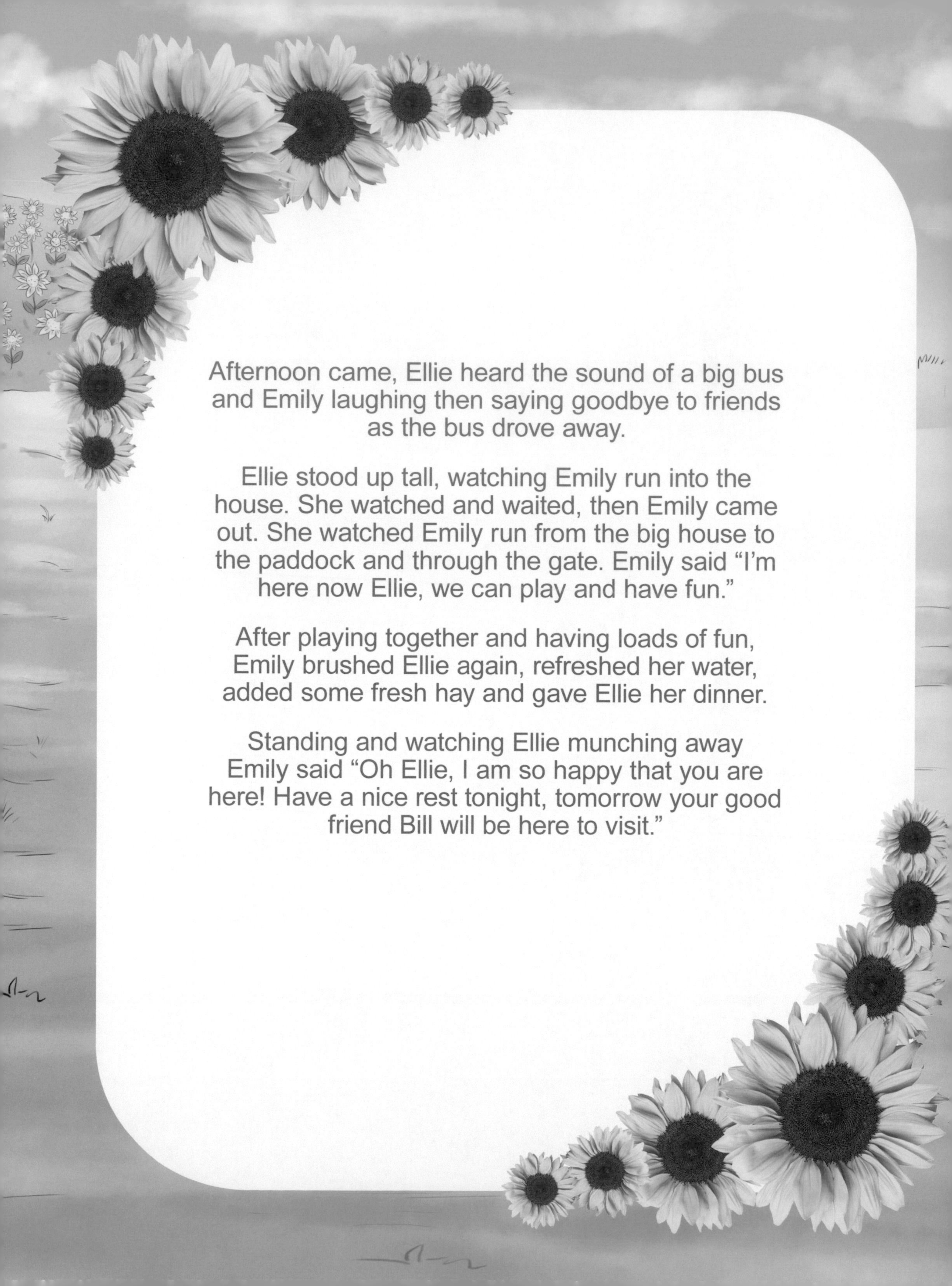

Afternoon came, Ellie heard the sound of a big bus and Emily laughing then saying goodbye to friends as the bus drove away.

Ellie stood up tall, watching Emily run into the house. She watched and waited, then Emily came out. She watched Emily run from the big house to the paddock and through the gate. Emily said “I’m here now Ellie, we can play and have fun.”

After playing together and having loads of fun, Emily brushed Ellie again, refreshed her water, added some fresh hay and gave Ellie her dinner.

Standing and watching Ellie munching away Emily said “Oh Ellie, I am so happy that you are here! Have a nice rest tonight, tomorrow your good friend Bill will be here to visit.”

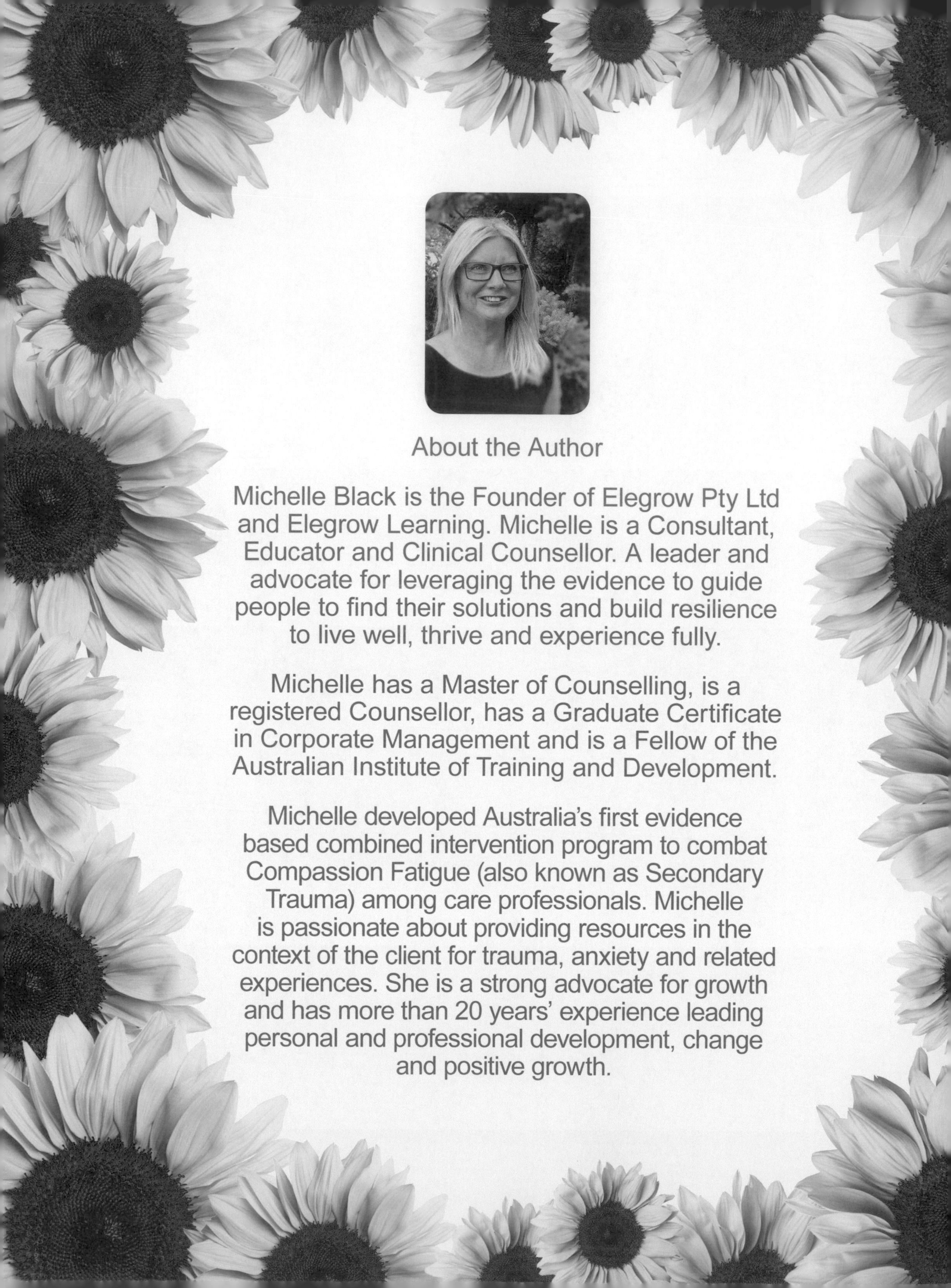

About the Author

Michelle Black is the Founder of Elegrow Pty Ltd and Elegrow Learning. Michelle is a Consultant, Educator and Clinical Counsellor. A leader and advocate for leveraging the evidence to guide people to find their solutions and build resilience to live well, thrive and experience fully.

Michelle has a Master of Counselling, is a registered Counsellor, has a Graduate Certificate in Corporate Management and is a Fellow of the Australian Institute of Training and Development.

Michelle developed Australia's first evidence based combined intervention program to combat Compassion Fatigue (also known as Secondary Trauma) among care professionals. Michelle is passionate about providing resources in the context of the client for trauma, anxiety and related experiences. She is a strong advocate for growth and has more than 20 years' experience leading personal and professional development, change and positive growth.

Printed in the United States
By Bookmasters